One day I found a DRAGON.

I hoped
it would stay.
I'd always wanted
A DRAGON!
But ... this little dragon looked
like it might set FIRE to the HOUSE.

So I did the OBVIOUS THING.

I wrote to the FIRE BRIGADE.

They would know what to do.

FINALLY,
I got a letter back.

I dried it off and opened it up.

So I did as I was told.
The dragon LOVED it. I could tell.

Later we were hungry.
I made my BEST
JAM SANDWICHES.

The dragon was not a fan.
But I knew just who to ask about dragon food!

I got a SPEEDY REPLY.

That day
the dragon ate
twenty-three STEAKS,
ten HAMS and half of my UMBRELLA!

His thank-you ROARS were VERY LOUD!

Maybe a bit
TOO loud...

I opened the letter VERY CAREFULLY.

DELIVERED BY · DELIVERED BY ·

CONTAINS IMPORTANT DOCUMENTS

Master Alexander
28 Draco Way
Beaconwood
B87 URN

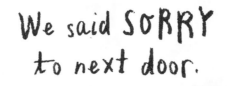

We said SORRY
to next door.

And my dragon TRIED to be quiet.

But it's hard when you're growing SO BIG in such a little house.

We needed help. PROFESSIONAL help.

The reply arrived just in time.

Mr. Alex
28 Draco Way
Beaconwood
B87 URN

AFTER 5 DAYS RETURN TO:

Bernard East

VIA AIR MAIL

So when the world was FAST ASLEEP,

we crept outside and SOARED into the sky.

We were HAPPY together.

I loved my dragon and I WISHED he could stay forever... But I don't think dragons are made to be PETS.

I wasn't sure what to do.
So I wrote to the WISEST person I knew.

She wrote back straightaway.

I showed my dragon
the letter and he
BEAMED AND SPARKLED.

We spent a final day together.

We didn't want to
say GOODBYE, but
we knew it was right.

I missed my dragon.

I would never forget him.

I hoped he would never forget me.

Then one day
I got some POST.

And it was ...

DRAGON POST!